TIMESCAPE TALES

CLIVE AUSTIN

Published by Sometimes Books

TIMESCAPE TALES
is also available as an ebook

* * *

CONTENTS

FOREWORD

Imagination and knowledge are powerful gifts. With them, worlds are created and destroyed.

For some, the stories that follow may be read for little more than simple entertainment. For others, deeper meaning may be sought. It is not for me to say which reading is correct. Such matters are for each individual to discern for themselves. What I will say is that if you do find any truths amongst them, take care when allowing them to unfold, for any truth you discover here will be your own.

All that remains then, is all that remains.

"Occasionally, tears in the fabric appear; fissures leading to places whose boundaries are not as stable or as uniform as our own.

Lingering too long here might be disorientating for some. Perspectives can shift dramatically - sometimes nudging observers toward realms beyond what is commonly considered to be sane.

In such places, the scale of time and space is shown for what it is, illusory. Be warned though, for such illusions are experienced as no less real.

For now, The Creature has yet to be tamed, The Children yet to be rescued, The Tyrant vanquished, The Spies unmasked, or the home of The Witch revealed."

O N E

"Somedays are just like that." He said.

"Like what?" She replied.

"You know." He said.

"I don't." She said. "Or I wouldn't have asked. What do you mean?"

"I suppose what I mean is…" He began.

"Yes?"

"I suppose what I mean is that some days…"

"Yes?"

"…some days it just feels like there isn't enough sun, or biscuits, or dancing."

"Ah." She said, carefully realigning the spheres that were levitating above the platform. They began to hum quietly. "That old one."

"Yes." He said, climbing onto the back of the chair and looking out of the window.

"…which means it's time to look out the window?" She said.

"Yes." He replied.

A small portal began to open at the midpoint between the spheres.

"Ah, windows." She sighed.

He stared at the people in the street and wondered what it would be like to be them.

"Are you wondering what it would be like to be them again?" She asked.

"Yes." He said. "Just a little."

"As long as you remember what it is like to be you."

She stood up and opened the basket.

"You mean the absence of sun and biscuits and dancing?" He replied.

"Yes." She said.

"Ah." He said. "That old one."

She smiled at him and turned back to the apparatus.

The inside of the room began to feel awkward, as it always did before a jump.

The portal opened to capacity and they peered in.

"Ready?" She asked.

"Always." He said.

T W O

The man had always been a seeker of truth.

He had also been a seeker of love, although his ability to acknowledge the full extent of this did not come until much later on in his life.

Fortunately for him it did not come too late.

The deep blue door, the path through the garden, the woman with the dogs he met there, the knowing embedded in the surprise of it all. All were details his future still had a firm hold on.

Sometimes people think they know what it is that they are, or what they are seeking, but in truth, they don't yet have the full picture. The result of this is that sometimes things don't feel like they quite add up. Life feels like it is missing a piece, some small detail, a simple fact - either about the person themselves, or the situation they are in. A simple truth that, once realised, causes a shift.

Such shifts can be profound. Sometimes life-changing.

The simple detail the man had been missing was the relationship between truth and love.

Knowing this, he told me, had changed everything.

"Full acceptance of the truth *is* love." He would say. "Because you cannot love anything truly until you accept it fully."

"Love without truth," He said, "Cannot be true love at all."

This realisation had caused him to see and experience a great many things in life very differently.

He realised that many of the things people manifested in their external reality were as much the result of how they met truth inside themselves as it was about how they met the world.

He said that the more truths people were able to accept on the inside, the more the world seemed to change for the better for them on the outside. Life seemed to line up more easily. People and things seemed to show up when they were needed. Life had a sort of flow, or people seemed to just flow with it, even at times when the currents seemed overwhelming.

When people got fearful or apprehensive and reacted to life by trying to control it, circumstances seemed to get the better of them.

At least that is how he came to see it.

By fully accepting the truth of life, he said, he came to love it more fully.

"Life is shaped by how we feel about it, as much as how our feelings are shaped by life." He said.

"When I accept the truth of something, I feel love for it, and it is the loving of it that changes it."

He said that there were some things he struggled to accept, so there were limits to what he could love, but for the most part, there was much more to love about life than he had once believed possible.

"Forgiveness." He said. "Is much underrated."

Although all this came with a warning.

"If I *try* to love the world because I want to change it, chances are, it will not change - it will see through the trick. I don't think the world - or people - take kindly to being manipulated in that way. But when I love without wanting anything in return, most of the time it will return to me something that I need, and often something I didn't realise I needed - or something I wanted - but not in the way I imagined. The world can be like that. It's like it knows what is best for you.

Another thing to be aware of, the thing that took me the longest time to realise, was that what I need doesn't always look like what I think I want. Sometimes you have to be prepared to let go of what you think you want in order to get what you need, and, sometimes, you only get what you need once you learn to let go of what you think want. And that can be very painful indeed.

At other times it will all remain a mystery, and that will be the truth you will be invited to accept.

Learn to love the unfolding mystery of your becoming." He said.

"When there is a part of me that tries to escape the truth of how I feel, that part can take control of my life. The act of accepting the truth is what returns choice back to me. When life is a struggle and I accept the struggle, I choose to love the struggle, that is loving life for what it is, not what I think it should be.

It is like going for a walk in a storm. Once you accept that you will be drenched to the bone by the time you reach your destination, each drop becomes a part of the journey and no longer an inconvenience to be avoided."

He said that most of the people who tried to change the world, who tried to control their environment or other people, did so because they were trying to control their own uncomfortable feelings.

"Most people don't want to feel bad." He said. "Who does? It's just that most of us have been going about it the wrong way. The more people there are trying to change the external world in order to change how they feel about themselves on the inside, the more chaotic it becomes because people are competing to change the external world in different ways. When people change their relationship to truth and to their lives on the inside, and act from that place, then the world changes in response to their acceptance of truth, not as a result of them trying to force their will upon it. It does not try to mould life or force it to be something that instinctually it is not. It allows it to become what it needs to be - it leaves it to actualise its own potential. This is what love is, because this is what loving does. That is why love is as powerful as it is. It's actually quite simple." He said. "But just because it is simple that does not make it easy.

Learning to trust that the ocean within and the ocean beyond are the same sea is a challenge for anyone who has grown up believing that they are nothing more than the shoreline between them."

The man said that it had taken him a good half of his life to piece all this together.

On the day he crossed the final threshold into this knowing he had been sitting in front of the Griffin, letting the warmth of the sun reach in through his skin and all the way down to his bones.

"There are lions and eagles everywhere here." He had remarked to his companion and she had agreed.

They had worked together for a while as spies, but only for the briefest time. They had explored rivers, and songs, and ancient carvings in wood and stone too.

By the time they reached the cabin though, all of these pasts were well behind them.

His companion, who was wise in the ways of many things, had led him outside to look over the view. Whilst there, she had placed in his hands some plants gathered from far-off places. She told him that if he chose to, he could ask questions of them - the sorts of questions he might not be able to ask of a person.

The idea of communicating with plants and trees was not beyond him. He was well aware that the food he ate and the air he breathed were all part of a wider conversation, a conversation that had been going on for a very long time indeed.

"I have been having these conversations all my life." He told her.

"Yes." She said, "But are you sure you have been listening?"

So he took the plants, asked his question, and listened.

It was not until the sun began to set that he heard the plants reply.

At first, they came as simple sounds and syllables, then, after a while, as simple words.

While he could translate these words into his own tongue, they were not words he heard with his ears. They registered somewhere else in him, somewhere further back, somewhere ancient. Somewhere he realised had been left disused. This was not neglect on his part, but rather ignorance - he just hadn't realised that place was there.

He was beginning to see that the language he was hearing was woven through the fabric of all things. It was so full of truth and wonder and bliss and love that each word felt like it contained an entire lifetime of knowing.

"These words are seeds of life." The wise woman had told him. "Each one is full of potential."

The more he listened the more his heart opened. It bloomed in him like a mighty flower; a thousand petals over countless layers, peeling back, again and again. All that he had been holding onto that had become unnecessary was offered the freedom to leave.

Much of it did, and as it dissolved away, the spaces within him opened more.

Broader.
Deeper.
Wider.
Brighter.

Each layer was like this he said; each question and each answer, eroding all of the artificial structures that had been framing him for so long.

What remained was purer, simpler, more refined: A crystal clear river flowing gently through a translucent sea.

He realised that some people spent entire lifetimes waiting and wanting and seeking but never finding because they looked in every corner for that which they sought but into the deepest realms of themselves; ancient places where echoes of forests and mountains they had never known lived on.

The man, being the seeker he was, had looked high and low for love without realising that the broadest, deepest, widest, brightest, and truest sense of it, had been with him all along.

"The world is full of cliches for a reason." He said.

"Realising the truth of them is not the same as knowing they exist."

When the following morning came, he and the wise woman left the cabin and went their separate ways.

The man took the knowledge he had gained and did his best to share it with those whom he believed might prosper from it most.

It soon became clear to him that such knowing is not an easy thing to share. So he let go of trying and allowed life just to be as it was.

Because the ocean within reflects the ocean beyond, it will come of little surprise to some that it was very soon after this that he found a match for himself in the world.

When he met the woman from the garden for the third time he shared with her a story. It was a story he had shared before with many others but it had never been received in the way the woman received it then.

It was the story of the unknown becoming; the unfolding mystery that lives in and between all moments.

She had smiled, "That is my favourite story." She told him.

"The thing about true love," He said. "Is that it is obvious. You can accept the truth of the other as if it were your own. Which is why it is difficult to find until you have found it for yourself."

It was not long after that they gathered themselves and their belongings together in the same place.

It was then their adventure began.

THREE

Even though they could not speak the language, it was clear that the being charged with the task of directing them was not impressed.

On reflection, they liked to believe that, had they been able to interpret its gestures more clearly, the answer they may have finally received would have been very different from the one they actually did. At least that is what they told themselves when they came to evaluate the situation later on.

Once ejected from the room they had pretty much been left to their own devices. It was only the pointing finger and smile of a compassionate stranger that saved them from entering the wrong door again.

They looked at the slips of paper in their hands and up at the sign.

"I guess this is it." He said.

"How long do you think it will take?" She asked.

"Forever I imagine."

They sat down to wait, perturbed by the incessant rain and lack of cushions.

"Let's play a game." She said.

He shrugged. "Sure. Why not. What game did you have in mind? Not the one where you throw things at me and I have to dodge them?"

"No." She said. "Not this time."

He looked around for places to hide just in case she changed her mind. "What one then?" He asked.

She paused.

"Would you rather." She said.

He could hear something in the distance roaring. The sound of the rain made it hard to tell what it was. From where he sat it could have been a wild creature or a heavy mechanical device trying to lift itself into the air.

"O.k." He said. "Do you want to go first?"

She nodded.

"Would you rather be here with me, or would you rather be somewhere else on your own?" She asked.

He gave her one of his looks. "But you already know the answer to that question." He said.

"Maybe." She said coyly. "But I might want to hear you say it again."

The unknown distant roar was eaten up by increasing rain. It was more like a waterfall than rain. He was beginning to wonder where it was all coming from.

He knew that this was all part of the game.

"I would rather be here with you." He said.

She smiled.

"You win."

F O U R

It was another time. A time before.

"Well let's hope you get somewhere with it."

The words threatened to land in her, familiar and heavy. The feeling had been so familiar for so long that she could not remember a time without it. It was so familiar that the feeling was how she had come to believe things were.

Although all that was about to change.

She would never know exactly what it was that caused the shift. She would never feel the need to know, although she would feel grateful that it did.

"Well let's hope you get somewhere with it."

This time, rather than react, she paused, and then she found herself saying…

"What exactly do you mean?"

The words fell out of her mouth without thinking. It was such an obvious question, but obvious questions, like obvious things, can remain hidden in plain sight for years, masked by the assumptions that get layered over them.

There was a realisation that arrived with the question too. She never bothered to question why, something just shifted and she went with it.

It was like slotting a puzzle piece into place, but rather than feeling like she had discovered the missing piece from a larger picture, it was the other way around. She had never thought to question that the part she had been carrying for so many years was a part of anything else at all. She had always assumed that it was something complete, rather than a piece of something that had been left incomplete. When she found the empty space, she had reached out without thinking and the piece had slotted into it with a satisfying click. Then the picture was whole and everything made sense.

"Well, I mean, let's hope you make some money from it." He said.

Every time she had heard those words before it was like being on top of a fast-moving vehicle that brakes suddenly. The momentum had always flung her forward, out of control to tumble and crash and bruise no matter what, but this time something was different. This time the picture was clear. This time, instead of being flung uncontrollably to the ground she realised that she had a choice not to land at all, and in choosing not to land, she flew.

"Do you realise." She said. "That every time you say something like that, that you 'hope I will get somewhere with it,' you miss the point. Not just the point about me or the point about my life but life in general. All of the things I do I value because they are part of life and life is creation. Creation is *in* me, and it *is* me. Every time you measure that against how much money I might make you miss the point of it all. To create, to refine that creation to the point that it feels good, and right, and true, and beautiful, or simple - or just complete - that is my success - that is what fulfils me because it is life fulfilling its potential through me - which is one and the same thing. When you ultimately frame my efforts in terms of money all you do is show me that you don't see this. You are telling me that the final measure of value in me conspiring with creation is monetary, and that is what matters most."

"But you need money to live." He replied.

"Maybe I do, but does life *need* money to live?" She stated the words calmly. "I've got no issue with making money from selling what I create, but that is not the purpose of creating for me, nor is it the measure of my creations' worth - not their true worth. Money is a secondary measure of value - it is someone else's value of my creations' worth - not mine. I show you the things I make - the creatures, the artefacts, the forms, the symbols. When I share these things, and all that pours out of me, I am sharing something from deep within. They are not created as commodities to be brokered or assets in which to invest. They are reflections of my soul and, in some way, the soul of life. Do you realise that all these years I have been feeling like a failure because whenever you ask me how I am and I tell you, your final measure of what

I say is always monetary, and I have been secretly measuring myself by that standard for years, and I didn't even realise until now, and it is all because I wanted you to love me for who I am, not because of what I create, or what I earn, or what I do."

With the words released, with the feelings felt, she became physically lighter. She even began to glow. If you had looked closely enough, you would have seen that she had begun to lift off of the ground, ever so slightly.

"Creation is creation." She continued. "It is sacred, and it is a magical act. It is a magical act because where there was nothing before, then there is something. Sure, I could design things and sell them for profit, but there is no life in that for me - to create something and then measure it according to the profit I could gain from its sale would be a type of madness. To create something just to sell, that would make it artificial and contrived. When I create I am as much a passenger as I am the one who steers the boat. The market cannot measure the value of creation, because the value of creation is beyond our ability to measure in its fullness. The deep vaults out of which these treasures flow remains a mystery to me, and I suspect it always will. That is the truth of it."

She paused.

A brightly coloured bird flew down and landed on the ground between them. A spark of gold glinted as it blinked a mechanical eye. It looked at them both, noticing that its creator was now levitating a good wings width above the ground.

The old man nodded and smiled inoffensively. "Oh well." He said. "Let's hope you make some money out of it all the same. It would be such a shame to let all that effort go to waste."

She smiled an inoffensive smile in return. "Yes." She said. "It would."

F I V E

Hauled free of the tide, the upturned boat left safe in the hollow of a dune, he strode into the desert with bare feet.

The summer had been too long and too short by equal measure. To make things worse, he was lost again.

After walking for what felt like an age he finally reached the ruins of a large house. It was clear that the house had once been stately, although how it had ended up in the dunes of the desert was something of a mystery. Either it had made its own way there, or the desert had come to it. Either way, it was strangely misplaced.

It looked to have been gutted by fire many years before.

Inside, in the centre of the house, in what he assumed were the remains of a once impressive entrance hall, a tree had taken root. Judging by the size of its trunk the house must have been without a roof for well over a hundred years, maybe more. The bare branches of the tree looked lifeless.

The only clue as to his whereabouts was what looked to be some sort of a map, etched into the carbonised surfaces of the house's walls. It ran like a labyrinth across the surfaces of the entire building.

The topography the map defined was complex, and while drawn on a two-dimensional surface, when viewed at certain angles, it appeared holographic.

Whatever the map was a map of he got a very clear sense that it was not just a representation of the physical realm he was in. It seemed to hint that there was a lot more going on in that space than the limits of his senses were able to register. The image of it seemed to be whispering to him of another reality, but it was so faint.

Straining to make sense of it he could see that parts of the map looked like they were pointing to more than three dimensions. From one position he thought he counted up to thirteen; the etched lines folding in, around, beyond, and between each other. He felt disoriented by it, dizzy and occasionally a little sick. He had to keep closing his eyes and holding onto something to regain his balance and composure.

"What can it all mean?" He asked under his breath.

As if in reply, a piece of plaster, already peeling, fell stiffly to the floor and shattered. Stepping briskly aside to avoid it, the map suddenly fell into relief.

It was like being able to see all things in all directions simultaneously. Like someone had pulled aside the curtain on creation and all of the working mechanisms behind it had been exposed. No less beautiful, or tragic, or magical, or mundane - just clearer.

He smiled. It was suddenly obvious where he was.

In that moment the map, along with the ruins of the old house, began to crumble about him. In the end, all that remained was a wide band of white dust encircling both him and the tree.

The tree, which only moments before had looked so dead, was now covered in the buds of tiny leaves.

"Well." He said. "Here we are."

S I X

If The Creature was renowned for anything it was for collecting something of the essence of people's lives in exchange for the fulfilment of some wish or desire.

It is fair to say that for those people who entered into such contracts, The Creature was considered to be more infamous than renowned.

The essence The Creature sought was commonly referred to as the soul; that part of a person which grows through life but is not the body alone.

Why The Creature valued this essence so much remained a mystery.

The most popular theory was that The Creature sought to collect the souls of others because it had no soul of its own, but no one could be certain of this for sure. What was clear was that it sought to claim them wherever it could, and by whatever means.

The boy, whom this particular tale concerns, was very young for one who might consider making such a deal, but The Creature, being what it was, was all too ready to take him at his word.

"In exchange for my soul." Said the boy. "Anything I want, I will have."

While the circumstances that led the boy to want to make such a deal were never made clear to me, what was clear was that the boy's motivation seemed less to do with greed and more to do with power. This desire was not for power over others but for power over his own desires, for he felt them so keenly that they threatened to overwhelm him at every turn.

The boy performed a ritual to seal the deal and then went off into life, reassured that he would get all that he wanted when he wanted it, and no longer have to suffer the pain of unfulfilled desires anymore.

As time passed, and the deeper into manhood he strode, the more it became unclear as to if he ever really got what he wanted at all.

He knew that sometimes he did. Sometimes he got exactly what he wanted, and with unerring speed and accuracy. It was just that it never seemed consistent.

Sometimes he would want for things that didn't turn up until some time later. Sometimes, when they finally did, he would have forgotten that he had ever wanted them at all. Worse still, sometimes they would show up at the exact moment as something else he had wanted, and the two things would end up in conflict. Often to such a degree that they would cancel each other out and he would be left with neither.

There were also times when he found himself wanting things in a less than positive frame of mind; at times when he wasn't thinking or feeling straight. This meant that he would sometimes end up having experiences he would live to regret.

He felt like The Creature had planned it that way - if such a thing were at all possible - that it was all part of some clever joke being played out at his expense. The worst thing was, was that he knew that the only person he could blame for the situation he found himself in, was himself.

A sense of emptiness grew within him, an emptiness that filled a space where he assumed his soul should be. This emptiness, he believed, was the result of never being sure if he had ever really earned what he had because he was never sure when the results of his actions were his. As such he never felt truly satisfied or fulfilled.

Someone had once told him to "Be careful what you wish for because you just might get it." These words had become more and more meaningful with every passing year.

Deep down he felt more and more like a fool and he resolved that the deal with The Creature had been a bad idea all along. If this was what exchanging his soul had cost him, he no longer wanted any part of it.

He knew The Creature did not have a reputation for negotiation, quite the opposite in fact. He resolved to make his appeal to it nonetheless.

Once he had worked out what he would say, he summoned The Creature with immediate effect.

He explained to The Creature that he had made a terrible mistake; that he had been too young and too naive to have made such a deal in the first place.

He told The Creature that his naivety had tricked him into believing that fulfilment was to be gained from acquiring what he desired.

He said time had taught him that fulfilment was achieved through the act of engaging in life. That fulfilment was realised through the effort of turning one's potential into something real.

The Creature had just stared at him.

What The Creature didn't know was that the man had desired wisdom, and that above all else this one desire had never changed in him.

"All know your reputation creature." He continued.

The Creature stared at him, unblinking.

"I made a deal with you." He said.

The Creature nodded.

"I made a deal with you that in exchange for my soul, that anything I want, I will have."

"Well," said the man. "There is only one thing that I want now, and when I have it our contract will be settled."

The Creature stared at him.

"What's more, I want it with immediate effect."

The Creature nodded.

"I want my soul back." Said the man.

With that, The Creature vanished.

It was unclear at first whether anything had changed at all. This simple fact caused the man to doubt if The Creature had ever claimed his soul in the first place. In fact, he wondered if The Creature had ever claimed anyone's soul. He wondered if The Creature had any power whatsoever. That perhaps the only power it had was letting people believe it had any power over them at all.

Whatever the truth of it was, from that moment on, the man's life changed for the better. Although he still had conflicts and challenges to face, each and every victory, along with his soul, now felt like his own.

SEVEN

She had grown up in a cult of three.

Her parents never shared their practices with the outside world, choosing to keep their rituals and traditions private.

Their practices had been sober and temperate affairs that mainly revolved around the preparation of food and negotiating what distractions they would engage in during the long evenings.

From the earliest of her days she had longed for change, but the older she grew the more she found herself having a strange appreciation for the past.

Despite the threat of nostalgia, she appreciated the charm and simplicity those early times had to offer; a charm and simplicity that seemed lost to the age in which she eventually found herself.

One night she had dreamt that her mother had come to her and said, "When you are older the world will change and you will have to form your own ways or run the risk of falling into the past with us."

On waking she told her mother of the dream and of her plan - that at the first possible opportunity she was going to leave and create a world in which she would live true to the ways that were hers.

"If you want pudding." Her mother had told her in reply. "You'll have to finish your main."

For the longest time she wondered if her mother's response had been a symbolic one. If food or eating was in some way code for the optimal approach to experiencing life. She eventually resolved that her mother had simply been imparting functional advice about the order in which to eat her meals. She saw what happened to people when they only ate pudding so she got it. While she may have been a maverick, she was no fool.

This much of life was clear to her then.

Of the intervening years she remembered little.

Mostly she remembered people complaining about the lack of cushions and how uncomfortable their cages were. She had never really understood why people got into the cages in the first place, let alone why they built them.

Her parents had told her that was just the way things were; the way things had always been. That she would do well to just accept the facts and get on with life like everyone else.

Unlike the majority of her peers she never accepted this as a valid proposition. Life meant something very different to her indeed, something that was almost the exact opposite of cages, regardless of how many cushions they might contain.

When the time came to build her own she simply ignored all requests and commands to do so. This was met with widespread disapproval, none of which bothered her.

At the first possible opportunity she bought the sturdiest pair of walking boots she could find and took off into the world carrying all she owned on her back.

When the time came to create her own ways she followed the advice of the mother who had come to her in dream.

She travelled many miles and had many adventures, and while she never once regretted leaving, on occasion, she did regret eating too much pudding.

E I G H T

None of them expected the apocalypse, not on a beach day. All that planning gone to waste. The children's old wetsuits would have been fine for another year after all. Still, how were they to know.

No one had touched the picnic either.

She thought of the eggs boiling; the moment of removing them from the water.

It had always felt like such an effort to get the perfect boiled egg. How time always seemed to drag in the waiting. She could see the second hand ticking across the sky, giant footsteps beating out their rhythm across the sand.

The worst thing about boiled eggs at a picnic, she thought, was not knowing how they had turned out until someone opens one, which could be hours from the point of their creation. All that anticipation.

She wondered how the eggs she had cooked that morning had turned out. She knew she would never know.

She looked down at the cooler, tempted to rush over and tear through them, one by one, just to find out. There must be something more significant she could be thinking she thought to herself. There must be a more meaningful way to spend your last moments on earth?

At least they would not have to contend with the threat of car sickness on the way home. At least there was that.

She looked at her husband.

He seemed to be doing remarkably well. The low-level anxiety he usually carried with him seemed to have disappeared. He seemed almost serene. No. He was serene.

Actually, he was relieved. The struggle that had become his life was now over. No more pitiful, demeaning, economic slavery. He was with his family, the sun was shining, the air was fresh and he was thinking of the very satisfying shit he had taken before they left. If there was a good day to die then this was as good a day as any.

The children were terrified and bemused in equal measure.

Thankfully, both had it in mind that death was much like a reset in a computer game, so the true impact of the situation was somewhat lost on them. Or not, depending on your point of view.

They all felt a strange sense of pride in being the only family in earshot not to scream when the final moments came.

The last sense of life they had was of the warmth of each other's bodies and the smell of the embrace they held themselves within.

That and a final word from the youngest child.

"mum?"

N I N E

"Some days are just like that." The heiress was flustered.

He tried to keep the boat at a safe distance. Close enough to hear her but far enough away to prevent it from catching alight.

An ember floated down into some of what soft furnishings remained, burning a small but noticeable hole in one of the cushions.

"Anyway." She continued, switching tack. "How are things with you?"

"Thing like, I suppose." He replied.

She scooped up another pail of water and hauled it onto the base of the blaze, bucket and all.

"Well, that's the last of them." She said.

"Are you sure I can't offer you a lift somewhere?" He asked her.

"Certain." She said. "It will burn itself out soon enough."

"Are you sure? It looks fairly fierce."

She shrugged. "It'll be fine." She said.

He had an urge to insist further but knew her well enough to know he had pushed far enough already.

"I'll see you soon." She said.

It was all that he could do not to look back.

Beyond the sound of the fire, a fragment of a letter, carried by an updraft, drifted down and landed at his feet. On it was written what remained of a heartfelt plea in a hand he didn't recognise.

It felt like some private memory into which it would have been impolite to pry so he picked it up and lay it carefully on the surface of the water.

He tried to reassure himself with the thought that some people just don't want to be saved, but couldn't help wondering if he should have done more.

He wrestled with the dilemma right up until he reached the shore, at which point he resolved that he had done all that was for him to do.

It was only then that he remembered where he had left his shoes.

T E N

Like a window with a view on an upturned world, the water around the tiny island on which the cabin sat did not move.

Not even a ripple. Perfectly still.

It was unnerving and unnatural.

The air was still too; no breeze. Nothing.

No sound either.

It was all so deafening.

It was as if all life had been drained from the place and the physical world seemed in no rush to reanimate existence at all.

The only things that moved and made a sound were the creaking planks on the boardwalk as they made their way cautiously toward the little hut.

It was no comfort. The last thing they wanted was to announce their presence. If The Witch was there then she would know they were coming, and if she knew they were coming she would know not to make a sound.

They were, in that moment, very, very afraid.

* * *

Many years before a sage had shared words of advice.

"Expect the unexpected." He had said.

Of course it was a cliche. The conversation had contained more than its fair share of them.

Perhaps it was because he had saved that specific one until last that the man had come away feeling such a weight in it.

It wasn't The Sage's voice, or his size, or his demeanour. He was not what you would call impressive or charismatic. There was, however, a calmness and a certainty in his ways that made him convincing.

"Expect the unexpected."

Perhaps it was the pause that The Sage had held onto before delivering the words that had given them more weight than they might normally have had.

Perhaps it was the surprise? The man had already claimed the silence that preceded the words as a parting gift.

There had been a knowing in The Sage's eyes too. A knowing that spoke of something impending. "Something is coming for you." They said.

"Expect the unexpected."

As the man had left The Sage had waited on the steps and then gently, but firmly, closed the door behind him. The man had got the distinct impression that it would be the last time he would see The Sage because of it.

To The Sage's credit the unexpected did indeed happen.

Many times in fact.

Thanks to his warning the man had been ready for it on the vast majority of those occasions.

The thing with the unexpected though, is that no matter how hard you try to prepare for it, there will be times when you will not be able to. This is what makes the unexpected what it is.

* * *

At the far side of the creaking boardwalk, on the tiny island of The Witch, with lumps in their throats, and their hearts trying to beat paths clean out of their chests, they kicked down the door and flooded the hut with light and fury.

To their surprise it was empty.

A note lay on the table.

On it, a single word, written in The Witch's hand.

'suckers'

It said.

Which, if you knew The Witch as well as they did,
would have come as no surprise at all.

E L E V E N

"You're new here." She said.

"I'm not entirely sure where *here* is." He replied.

"That's alright." She said. "You don't need a name for it."

"I suppose not… what are those children doing?"

"They're waiting for the future." She said.

"Oh." He replied. He hadn't expected her to say that.

She read his surprise with ease.

"I know." She said. "Not everything here is as straightforward as it seems."

They walked some distance, to what felt like the edge of something. It was there that she told him it was time for her to return to her friends.

"Well, it was nice meeting you..." He offered her his hand; a gesture of gratitude.

She looked at it, then to his eyes, and then back to his hand. She held it softly.

"....Truth." she said. "My name is Truth."

That's an unusual name he thought.

"Yes." She said, reading his mind. "It is an unusual name."

"Oh, I wasn't…" He began.

"It's alright." She interrupted. "It's an unusual name where you are from so it's only natural you would think so." She smiled. "Where I am from, it is less so."

"Ah." He said wondering where it was she was from.

She was ahead of him. "Not here." She said.

"You read my mind again." He replied.

"It's hard not to." She replied.

A large creature with shaggy fur and long stalk-like legs passed by, close enough to cause the man to feel a little anxious.

"They're harmless." She said watching the creature stride away.

The man let out a little sigh.

"Some of the creatures here are less so." She said turning back to face him.

The man felt suddenly unnerved.

"You'll be fine." She said reassuringly. "You can spot most of them a good way off. Plenty of time to get out of the way."

"Most of them?" He added.

"Mmhmm." She said.

"What about the others?"

"Are so fast it would be over before you knew it."

"Is that supposed to be reassuring?" He asked.

"No." She said. "Just factual."

He swallowed hard. She smiled.

"Anyway, all this chit-chat, I really must get back."

She walked off but turned to give him a final wave.

"What do I do now?" He called out after her.

She turned and flung both arms up into the air "Whatever you like." She called back. Then, with a little hop, she skipped away.

A small mechanical bird landed at his feet. It looked up at him expectantly.

It was then he realised that he was standing on a shore between two great oceans.

"Right." He said, suddenly inspired. "I shall build a boat."

TWELVE

"I'm packed. I'm not taking much. Just some old letters and a spare notebook, just in case. I am taking the old nail too. The one that used to stick out of the floor, the one we stood on for months before realising it was a nail? It reminds me of those times. That and the value of perseverance."

"I remember." He replied. "It was hidden in the carpet." He remembered the painful surprise of all the times it had dug into his heel.

"There were so many portals there, and here there are so few. In some ways that seems like a good thing, but in others, well, I miss it, the choice."

She pulled the curtains across the window and the room darkened.

"I'm willing to bet that you don't miss the tyrants." He said.

She lifted the lid on the basket and the cat climbed in and sat down.

"…or the witches." He continued. "Although I do miss the spies, don't you?"

"Yes, I do miss the spies. But missing, not missing. wanting, not wanting. It was all so confusing for so many years. I prefer this, how we do it now."

"Just letting the mystery unfold?" He said.

"Yes." She replied. "Just letting the mystery unfold."

The cat meowed.

"Do you think you'll ever get tired of this?" She asked.

"Not if I get to keep doing it with you." He answered.

The cat purred.

"It's strange how the simplest of things can close the gates to other worlds." He said.

"…and open new ones." She smiled.

They instinctively reached out and took each other's hands.

The portal closed about them and they were gone, while, in the same moment, somewhere else, they had just arrived.

THIRTEEN

They took the green path to The Junction, travelling in pairs and threes, shifting between conversations. Telling jokes, setting challenges, pushing limits.

Some of them knew what all that vitality meant. Others, inclined to blindness or folly, just used it up as they went along.

It is hard to say which path was the right one. You can never really tell until the very end, and by then, well, by then it is generally too late. There are no choices left to be made. Having no choices left to make is generally what makes the end the end.

Regardless, they loved each other all the same.

They carried themselves in through the doors and claimed what was left of the evening as their own.

They were born to create and destroy themselves by equal measure. It's how they were. It's how they were made.

The shifting between conversations, the telling of jokes, the setting of challenges, the pushing of limits - all this continued, but now there was dancing, and drinking, and fighting, and kissing to be done as well.

Everyone was there except for the children, who, having recovered from the journey, were tucked up safe in bed, watched over.

Even The Witch was there. She was sat with some of the newcomers teaching them how to see ghosts. The parents, still bemused and baffled by the events of their day, were running completely on trust. They would never really know the part they had played in it all. Which was probably for the best.

The artist was planting a garden of images in the far corner and laughing with her best friend about something they had found in one of the bushes.

The Creature was there too, surprisingly. Mostly it stared. Occasionally someone would approach it, out of politeness more than anything, but no one stayed with it for long. One of the girls spent a good while stroking it. It's hard to say whether it appreciated the attention or not.

The spies may or may not have been there too.

A boat was moored at the edge of the garden and a portal had been left open near the crossing, just in case.

When the night was closer to dawn than it had been to sunset they began to leave.

A handful returned to the house.

Conversations worth having that had fallen apart in the wake of their journey were rekindled.

Revelations were shared.

Somewhere they could hear love being made.

In the end, only three remained.

I shall leave it to you to imagine which three.

They made a small fire in the garden and beneath the stars they told each other tales.

This was what life was like at the end of the world.

Around glowing embers, as the last of the flames licked at the golden wood, one of them told the final story of the night.

PARALOGUE

"In the end, we will only ever have made the choices that we did. As such, no one escapes their destiny."

They looked up at the stars.

"There is so much that we do not know, so much that we can never predict for. We are bound by it, and to it, this continuous, unfathomable moment of becoming, and yet, we still have agency - we still have choice - or at the very least we have the illusion of it."

They could still feel the warmth of the fire.

"In the beginning there was nothing." He began.

"Out of the nothing, there came a something.

The something expanded into the nothing
and kept getting bigger,

and bigger,

    and bigger,

and bigger,

until one day,

there lived a boy.

The times in which the boy lived were hard and he travelled through the land carrying all of his belongings on his back.

The land in which the boy lived was divided by a vast wall that ran for as far as anyone knew - and further.

The boy had lived on both sides of the wall and found that whatever side of the wall he was on, the people who lived there always seemed to have unpleasant things to say about the people who lived on the other side.

This never sat easy with the boy for he found that whichever side of the wall he was on some of the people he met were pleasant and some of the people he met were not. Most people, he soon discovered, were, from time to time, a little bit of both.

As he travelled he shared stories. He would tell the people he met on his travels about the wonders he had seen and of the joys he had experienced.

Sometimes his stories were about what it was like on the other side of the wall.

Sometimes people listened.
Sometimes they did not.

Some of those who listened told him that, inspired by his stories, they would visit the other side of the wall to find out what it was like for themselves.

Whether they did or not, he never knew.

Either way, the thought alone pleased the boy because he had seen what ignorance could do.

By and large though people did not care to hear his stories. At best would just ignore him and he would move on of his own accord, at worse they would chase him out of town calling him names like 'troublemaker'.

Eventually, there came a day when, frustrated by the ignorance and lack of imagination that surrounded him, he decided that, rather than tell people what it was like on the other side of the wall, he would show them.

So he climbed up to the top of the wall, and piece by piece, block by block, stone by stone, he began to take it apart.

At first, the people watched. Most with open mouths, for such an act was unheard of.

Once they realised precisely what it was that he was doing, and that there were no signs he was going to stop, people would step in.

No faster than the boy could take the wall apart, the people around him began to rebuild it.

He tried again in different towns but it was always the same. Groups of people would gather, intrigued by his efforts, but no soon than they began to see a gap beginning to appear, up they would step and fill it back in, faster than he could take it apart.

Then the boy would either be chased out of town or would just move on somewhere else, each time feeling a little more disheartened and a little more dispirited.

* * *

There came a day when the boy was sitting on top of the wall wondering what to do next, wondering if, in fact, the only thing left for him left to do was sit on the wall and wonder what to do next, when a girl, about his age, climbed up and sat down beside him.

Like he, she too was carrying all she owned on her back.

As they talked she told him that, like he, she too had lived on both sides of the wall and, like he, she had become disheartened and dispirited from trying to share with people what she saw as the simplest of truths.

It was then she told him of her plan.

It was simple enough. She was going to walk along the top of the wall until she found the end of it: until she found the place where the wall no longer was.

The boy said that it was a brilliant idea and that they should travel together.

The girl agreed.

The boy suggested that they should leave straight away and that they should go *this* way.

"No." said the girl.

"We should go *that* way."

The boy insisted. The girl insisted.

Eventually, they flipped coins agreeing,

…heads this way, tails that.

The boy got heads. The girl got tails.

They paused for a moment.

Then they wished each other luck and off they went.

One this way.

                                        The other that.

The boy walked,

and walked,

and walked,

and walked,

and walked,

and walked,

and walked,

and walked,

and walked,
and walked,

and walked,

and walked,

and walked,

and walked,

and walked,

and walked,

and walked,

for so long
and so far
that the boy,

eventually became a man.

Then one hot day,
far off in the distance,
he saw a figure on the wall
walking towards him.

It was a woman.

She too, like him, was carrying all
of her belongings on her back.

When they met they asked each other…

"Where have you come from?"

To which the other replied…
"Very, very far away."

And then they asked each other...

"Where are you going?"

To which the other replied...

"To the end of the wall...."

The man looked at the woman.

And the woman looked at the man.

And the man recognised that the woman was the girl.

And the woman recognised that the man was the boy!

And then they hugged.

And when they finally stopped hugging they sat down together,
and they talked,
and they laughed,
and they cried,
and they hugged again.

And then they ate,

and then they slept,

deep into,
and through the night.

The next day they walked along the wall together.

I cannot remember if they walked this way or that. I do not even know for how long they walked.

What I do know is that they walked until they found a place they both remembered, a place that they both agreed to love.

It was there they stopped, and wearing smiles, piece by piece, they began to take the wall apart.

After many, many, many, many, many hours work, they stood back and looked at the space they had created and, in that space, they imagined their lives together.

It was there they lived until the ending of their days…

…or thereabouts.

I cannot tell you if they lived happily ever after or not as that much of the story was never told to me.

I think it is fairly easy to imagine that they did.

And that is the end of the story.

Other than to say that over time other gaps appeared in the wall. It is impossible to say what inspired them or who created them, only that people began to take the wall apart.

In time there were more gaps than there was wall.

Of course, some people liked the wall, they said it made them feel safe. As such, in some parts of the land the wall remained.

In some parts of the land the wall grew even higher.

For the most part though the wall all but disappeared.

The something continued expanding into the nothing (or so I am told).

Some people forgot.

Some remembered.

Some girls became women,

some boys became men,

and a few of them

found

each

other."

By the end of the story the dawn was washing up on the sky in pale hues. The stars were going out one by one and the first birds had begun to sing.

They sat in silence amid the warm glow of it all.

When the fire was mostly ash they went inside, drank tea, and made breakfast.

After they had eaten they went out into the world.

People passed them by, unaware of the adventures unfolding within them still.

That was the way of it they told me.

And that is the way of it still.

Ingram Content Group UK Ltd.
Milton Keynes UK
UKHW010929260423
420810UK00001B/134

9 798215 4226